S0-AAK-116

The Berenstain Bears' NURSERY TALES

The very first stories
cubs like to hear
are the stories their parents
used to hold dear.

That's how Small Bear
became a great fan
of THE THREE BEARS, THE LITTLE RED HEN,
and THE GINGERBREAD MAN.

A FIRST TIME BOOK®

THE BERENSTAIN BEARS

Copyright © 1973 by Stanley and Janice Berenstain. All rights reserved under International and Pan-American Copyright Conventions. Published in the United States by Random House, Inc., New York, and simultaneously in Canada by Random House of Canada Limited, Toronto. ISBN: 0-717-28190-6 Library of Congress Catalog Card Number: 73-1901. Manufactured in the United States of America. 67890 A B C D E

NURSERY TALES

Stan & Jan
Berenstain

Random House 🏠 New York

The Three Bears

Once upon a time there was
a little girl named Goldilocks who
liked to walk in the woods.

She liked to look
at the ferns.

She liked to smell
the flowers.

She liked to chase
the butterflies.

She also liked
to open doors.
One day, she came
to a house deep
in the dark woods.

As bold as you please, she opened the door and walked in.

She saw three bowls of porridge on the table — a great big one, a middle-sized one, and a wee baby one.

What she did not see was that she was in the house of the three bears.

So she tasted the porridge in the great big bowl. Ouch! It was too hot! She tasted the porridge in the middle-sized bowl. Ooh! It was too cold! Then she tasted the porridge in the wee baby bowl. Yum-m! It was just right!

And she ate it all up!

Next, Goldilocks tried sitting in the three bears' chairs. Umfph! The great big one was too hard! Squish! The middle-sized one was too soft! Ummm! The wee baby one was just right!

But suddenly—crash! It broke all to pieces!

Then Goldilocks went upstairs to try the beds. First she tried Papa Bear's bed. Yuch! It was too scratchy! Then she tried Mama Bear's bed. Ugh! It was too lumpy! Then she tried wee little Baby Bear's bed. Aah! It was just right! And soon she was sound asleep.

While she was sleeping, the three bears came home.

They looked at their bowls of porridge.

"Someone's been tasting my porridge!" roared Papa Bear in a great big voice.

"Someone's been tasting *my* porridge!" said Mama Bear in a middle-sized voice.

"Someone's been tasting *my* porridge," cried Baby Bear in a wee little voice, "and ate it all up!"

They looked at their chairs.

"Someone's been sitting in my chair!" Papa Bear roared.

"Someone's been sitting in *my* chair!" said Mama Bear.

"Someone's been sitting in *my* chair," wailed wee little Baby Bear, "and broke it all to pieces!"

Then they went upstairs to look around. Papa Bear roared again. "Someone's been lying in my bed!"

And Mama Bear said, "Someone's been lying in *my* bed!"

"Someone's been lying in *my* bed," shouted Baby Bear, "and here she is!" And, sure enough, there was Goldilocks sleeping cozily in Baby Bear's wee little bed.

All that roaring and shouting woke up Goldilocks.

When she saw the angry bears looking at her, she jumped out of bed, climbed out the window, and ran out of the woods.

Never again was she quite so bold about opening strange doors deep in the dark woods.

The Little Red Hen

One day, when the little red hen was scratching around for food, she found a grain of wheat. Instead of eating it right then and there, she turned to the other animals in the barnyard and said, "Who will help me plant this wheat?"

"Not I," said the duck.
"Not I," said the cat.
"Not I," said the pig.

"Then I shall plant it myself," said the little red hen. And she did.

The wheat sprouted
and grew into a tall stalk.
"Who will help me cut the
wheat?" she asked.

"Not I," said the duck.
"Not I," said the cat.
"Not I," said the pig.

"Then I shall cut it
myself," said the little red
hen. And she did.

At the top of the wheat was a large cluster of grain. "Who will help me thresh the wheat?" she asked.

"Not I," said the duck.
"Not I," said the cat.
"Not I," said the pig.

"Then I shall thresh it myself," said the little red hen. And she did.

Soon she had a sack of grain.
"Who will help me take the wheat
to the mill?"

"Not I," said the duck.
"Not I," said the cat.
"Not I," said the pig.

"Then I shall do it myself,"
said the little red hen. And she did.

The mill ground the wheat into flour for baking bread. "Who will help me bake the bread?" asked the little red hen.

"Not I," said the duck.
"Not I," said the cat.
"Not I," said the pig.

"Then I shall have to bake it myself," she said. And she baked a big round loaf of bread.

"Now, who will help me eat the bread?" she asked.

"I will!" said the duck.
"I will!" said the cat.
"I will!" said the pig.

"Oh, no," said the little red hen. "You did not help me plant the wheat. You did not help me cut the wheat. You did not help me take it to the mill, and you did not help me bake it. So you will not help me eat the bread. I will eat it myself." And she did.

It was delicious!

The Gingerbread Man

Once, in a little old house in the woods, there lived a little old woman and a little old man.

While the little old man was outside in the yard, the little old woman was inside baking a gingerbread man with currants for eyes and raisins for buttons.

Before she could take it out of the pan, the gingerbread man jumped up, bounced out the door, and ran down the path.

"Stop! Stop!" cried the little old woman and the little old man, running after him into the woods.

But the gingerbread man laughed, and said,

"Run, run, as fast as you can!
You can't catch me,
I'm the gingerbread man!"

He ran past a long-eared rabbit and a little brown bear.

"Stop! Stop!" called the surprised rabbit and the hungry little bear.

But the gingerbread man laughed again, and said,

"Run, run, as fast as you can!
You can't catch me,
I'm the gingerbread man!
I ran away from the little old
*   woman and the little old man,*
And I can run away from you!
*   I can, I can!"*

Next he ran past a woodcutter, who dropped his ax and joined the chase.

The gingerbread man even laughed at the woodcutter.

"Run, run, as fast as you can!
You can't catch me,
I'm the gingerbread man!
I ran away from the little old
    woman and the little old man,
    the long-eared rabbit
    and the little brown bear,
And I can run away from you!
    I can, I can!"

And he did, until he came to a stream that was too wide to cross without getting wet and soggy.

"Jump on my tail!" offered a sly fox, wading into the stream.

"Since your tail is so far from your mouth, I shall!" said the gingerbread man. And he straddled the tip of the fox's nice dry tail for the ride across.

But the stream was deep, and soon the fox's tail got wet. "Jump on my back!" said the sly fox.

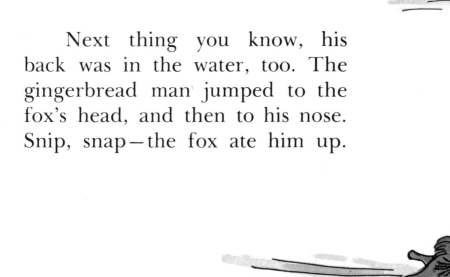

Next thing you know, his back was in the water, too. The gingerbread man jumped to the fox's head, and then to his nose. Snip, snap—the fox ate him up.

But, after all, that's what
a gingerbread man is for!

The End